P9-DFB-395

This book belongs to

.........................................

# FAMILY LEARNING

from Dorling Kindersley

*The Family Learning mission is to support the concept of the home as a center of learning and to help families develop independent learning skills to last a lifetime.*

Editors: Bridget Gibbs, Fiona Munro
US Editor: Kristin Ward
Designers: Claire Ricketts, Lisa Hollis

Published by Family Learning
Southland Executive Park, 7800 Southland Boulevard, Orlando, Florida 32809

Dorling Kindersley registered offices:
9 Henrietta Street, Covent Garden, London WC2E 8PS

VISIT US ON THE WORLD WIDE WEB AT:
http://www.dk.com

Copyright © 1998 Dorling Kindersley Limited

All rights reserved. No part of this publication
may be reproduced, stored in a retrieval system,
or transmitted in any form or by any means, electronic,
mechanical, photocopying, recording, or otherwise without
prior written permission of the copyright owner.

ISBN 0-7894-3791-0

Printed and Bound in the USA
by Inland Press

# The
# Bear
# Who Wanted
# to Read

LEE DAVIS • Illustrated by SUSAN WINTER

FAMILY LEARNING

When Ben the bear first came to live with
Max and Jenny he was a little bit lonely.
Jenny was at school all day, and Max was at
preschool in the morning.

There were a few other toys in the bedroom, but they were either too big . . .

or too little . . .

or weren't any fun.

Ben picked up a book and looked at
the pictures inside, but that didn't
take very long. He wasn't sure what
books were for.
Maybe he could
make something
with them.

The little ones could
be building
blocks and
the great
big one
could be
a slide.

All the rest of the books could be put together
to make a path around the bedroom.

At bedtime, Ben found out what books were for. Jenny read Max a story about some animals who went sailing in a boat and found some treasure on an island. Ben thought it was wonderful. Magic.

When the story was finished, Max said, "Read me another one. Please, Jenny!" Yes, thought Ben, more magic please! "Another time," said Jenny. "It's time for sleep now." She turned out the light and got into her own bed.

Ben lay in the moonlight and thought about the story. He really wanted another one.

He got out of bed and went to the bookshelf. He chose a book, opened it, and waited.

Nothing happened. Ben turned a page, and then another page. By turning the pages one at a time, with the pictures the right way up, he could follow the story a little, but he couldn't make the story come to life the way Jenny had.

He didn't know what the words on the pages said.

Maybe I'll learn tomorrow, he thought. He climbed back into bed and went to sleep.

The next day, Jenny and Max got ready to go out as usual, but instead of staying at home, Ben went to preschool with Max.

Preschool was fun! The other children had brought their toys, too, and they all got to know each other.

Ben sat close
to Max while
he did some
counting
with colored
shapes . . .
and then some
drawing and
painting.

Next, the teacher read a story about a cat and
a mouse, and when it was over the children all
went outdoors to play. The toys stayed indoors.

Ben looked around. He saw some pictures on the wall. One, he noticed, was a cat, like the one he'd seen in the story. There was a word beside the picture.

"That must be the word for cat," said Ben,
climbing onto a chair to get a better look.
"It is," said a voice nearby, "**c a t** is cat."
Who said that, thought Ben, looking around.

The voice came from a tiger. "I know that word because I am a big wild cat," said the tiger. "You don't look like the animal that has the word 'cat' next to it," said Ben, getting off the chair.

"Well, tigers are cats," said the tiger.
"Do you know any other words?" asked Ben.
"I know my name," said the tiger. "It's Tim.
I can show you what it looks like, if you want."

Tim pointed to a pile of blocks on the floor, and beckoned for Ben to follow him.

"We can use the alphabet blocks," he said.

"All words are made from letters of the alphabet."

Tim found the letters he wanted. He put them in order from left to right.

"These say 'Tim'," he said. "The first one is a capital letter because names always start with capital letters, and Tim is my name. Can you find the letters to make the word 'tiger'?"

Ben looked at the word under the tiger picture on the wall. Then he found five blocks with letters on them that matched the letters in the word. He arranged the bricks to make the word 'tiger'. "That's me, Tim tiger!" said Tim.

apple    bear    cat    dog

"I wish I could make my name," said Ben.
"Well, I'm sure we can find the word 'bear',"
said Tim. "Look, there is a picture of a bear,
so that must be the word for bear underneath!"

Ben and Tim looked around for the block letters that matched the letters under the picture. When they'd spelled out 'bear', Ben was very pleased.

"But that's not my name," he said. "I wish I knew what letters I need to make 'Ben'."

"What letter do you think it starts with?" Ben asked.

"I'm not sure," said Tim, "but I think it's the same letter that 'bear' starts with. You're Ben the bear. It's the same sound, so it must be the same letter."

Tim searched through all the blocks until he found the one he was looking for. It was a capital **B**. "A capital **B** for the name 'Ben'," he said. "Now what comes next?"

hen

Ben looked at the pictures on the wall. There was one with the letters **h e n** underneath. "That's it!" he shouted. "Ben sounds like hen. So my name must use the letters **B e n**!"

Ben was almost too excited to look for the blocks. He knew which ones he wanted, but where were they? Finally, he found the two others he needed to spell out his name.

When the children came in from their break,
they were all very surprised to see their toys
sitting around some blocks. The blocks spelled
out the names 'Ben bear' and 'Tim tiger'.

The teacher was surprised, too.
"Oh, look," she said, "someone has made some
words out of blocks — can anyone tell me what
they say?"

Someone whispered,
  "Tim tiger."

But the teacher wasn't
  sure who it was.

Someone else said, "Ben bear."
But the teacher didn't see any
of the children speak.

Max collected his things and got ready to go
home. He picked up Ben and gave him a hug.

"Clever Ben bear," he whispered into Ben's furry ear. "You can help read the bedtime story tonight."